BEACH LANE BOOKS

An imprint of Simon & Schuster Children's Publishing Division • 1230 Avenue of the Americas, New York, New York 10020 • Copyright © 2011 by Keith Baker • All rights reserved, including the right of reproduction in whole or in part in any form. • Beach Lane Books is a trademark of Simon & Schuster, Inc. • For information about special discounts for bulk purchases, please contact Simon & Schuster Special Sales at 1-866-506-1949 or business@simonandschuster.com. • The Simon & Schuster Speakers Bureau can bring authors to your live event. For more information or to book an event, contact the Simon & Schuster Speakers Bureau at 1-866-248-3049 or visit our website at www.simonspeakers.com. • Book design by Sonia Chaghatzbanian • The text for this book is set in ITC Benguiat. • The illustrations for this book are rendered digitally. • Manufactured in U.S.A. • 0112 PCR • 5 6 7 8 9 10 • Library of Congress Cataloging-in-Publication Data • Baker, Keith, 1953– • No two alike / Keith Baker.—1st ed. • p. cm. • Summary: Follows a pair of birds on a snowflake-filled journey through a winter landscape, where everything everywhere, from branches and leaves to forests full of trees, is unique. • ISBN 978-1-4424-1742-7 (hardcover) • ISBN 978-1-4424-3602-2 (eBook)• [1. Stories in rhyme. 2. Individuality—Fiction. 3. Winter—Fiction.] I. Title. • PZ8.3.B175No 2011 • [E]—dc22 • 2010044659

no two alike

Keith Baker

Beach Lane Books
New York   London   Toronto   Sydney

No two snowflakes are alike,

almost, *almost* . . .

but not quite.

No two nests,
so soft and round,

no two tracks upon the ground.

No two branches, no two leaves,

no two forests, full of trees.

No two fences, long and low,

no two roads—where do they go?

No two bridges, wood or stone,

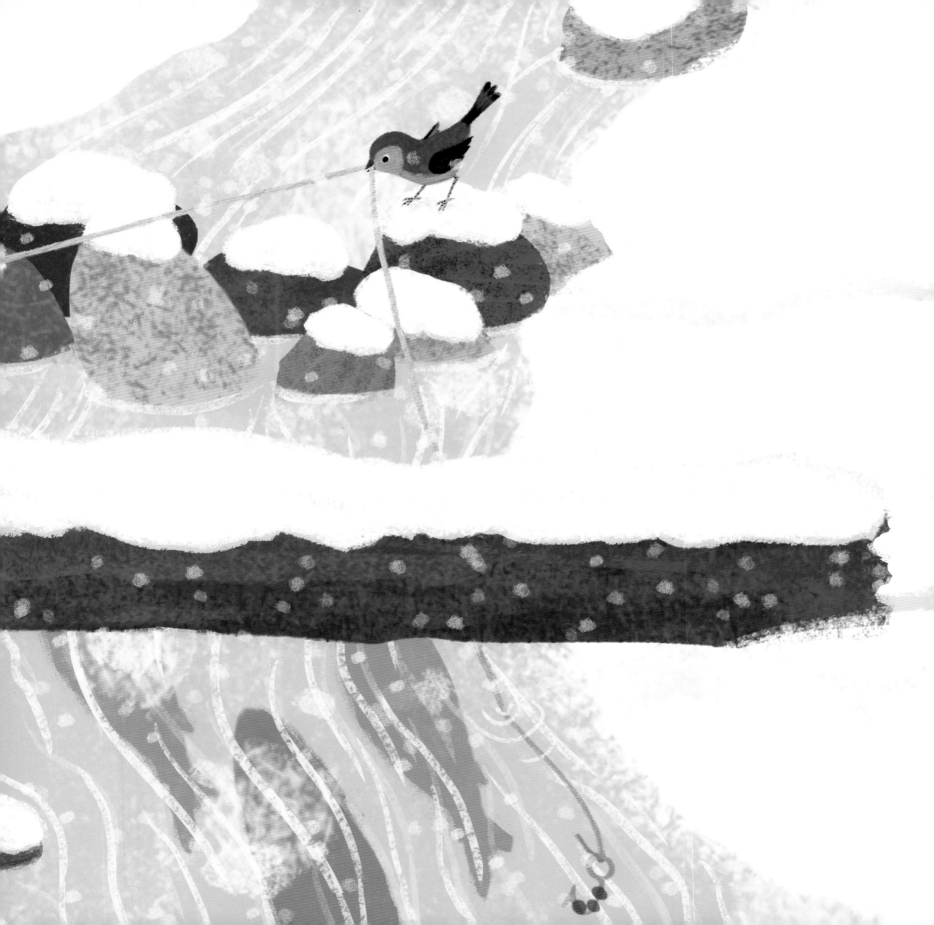

no two houses—
anyone home?

No two friends, large or small,
no two alike . . .

among you all!

Are we the same—

just alike?

Almost, _almost_ . . .

but not quite.